THE RED CARPET

THE
RED CARPET
Story and Pictures by Rex Parkin

A TRUMPET CLUB SPECIAL EDITION

Published by
The Trumpet Club
666 Fifth Avenue
New York, New York 10103

Copyright © 1948 by Macmillan Publishing Company,
a division of Macmillan, Inc.

The Trademark Dell® is registered in the U.S. Patent and Trademark Office.
ISBN: 0-440-84059-7

Reprinted by arrangement with Macmillan Publishing Company, Inc.
Printed in the United States of America
September 1989

10 9 8 7 6 5 4 3 2 1
UPC

TO INGRID

At the top of a hill, on La Salle Avenue,
Stood a little hotel. It was called the *Bellevue*.
It had green window boxes full of bright flowers . . .
A gaily striped awning to keep off the showers. . . .
On special occasions the doorman, in blue,
Rolled out a lovely red carpet too!

One day the head clerk
told the doorman, Jim West:
"I want the hotel
to look at its best.

The Duke of Sultana
is coming to stay.
Get busy and clean up
the front right away.

TELEGRAM

HOTEL BELLEVUE = CENTERTOWN
ARRIVING TODAY
WITH PARTY OF FOUR =
THE DUKE OF SULTANA =

Shine up the doorknobs,
and sweep up the floor,
Then roll out the carpet
right through the front door!"

So the doorman cleaned up
with a mop and a broom,
Then he put them away
in a little back room. . . .

He took out the carpet
they kept there in store
And laid it down gently
upon the smooth floor. . . .

He took off the string
and the covering, too,
Then he gave it a push
with the toe of his shoe.

Swiftly it rolled down the corridor floor,
Right through the lobby, and out through the door. . . .

Over the sidewalk where people were strolling.
Out to the curb—then . . .

IT KEPT RIGHT ON ROLLING!
Into the street, dodging buses and hacks,
Way out over the trolleycar tracks!

The doorman and clerk ran outside in surprise.
The doorman just couldn't believe his own eyes!
"I've rolled that red carpet out times by the score,
But nothing like *that* ever happened before!"

The chief clerk looked puzzled and scratched his head.
"You must have pushed it too hard!" he said.

In the meantime the carpet
   rolled on down the hill.

Second by second
   it rolled faster still!

Cars slammed their brakes on
   with loud grunts and squeals.

Dogs left their masters
   and barked at its heels!

The doorman ran after it
   shouting out "HEY!"

Everyone rushed
   to get out of the way!

Right by the traffic policeman it sped
　　Just as the light was turning to red.

The cop blew his whistle. It took no heed.
　　It was going fast now and gathering speed.

"Bless me!" cried Officer Mike O'Shea.
　　"The hotel's red carpet has run away!"

Then *zip*!—it dashed through the public square
And folks on the benches jumped up in the air!

To Tony Tortoni it gave such a start
He upset every pretzel he had on his cart!

It was speeding so fast that the wind whistled WHEEEEE!
As it whizzed past the statue of General Lee!

When it came to the park gates,
  the carpet swerved right.

Through the center of town
  it continued its flight.

It turned left at Pearl Street
and traveled down Main. . . .

At the corner of Plum Street
  it turned left again.

It weaved to and fro,
  in and out, like a thread . . .

And soon the whole city was colored bright red!

As it flashed by his office, the Mayor, Mr. Potts,
    Cried, "That carpet is tying this town into knots!
Arrest it at once! And restore peace and calm!"
    He pressed on a buzzer and gave the alarm . . .

And from station houses all over the place
Policemen poured out to take up the chase!

The carpet sped south
down De Witt Avenue.
Then it headed out east
along Route 22.

It was bowling along
like a hat in a gale
With a squad of policemen
hot on its trail!

They crouched on their cycles;
their faces were scowling!
Their motors were roaring!
Their sirens were howling!

Up hill and down dale, in great leaps and bounds,
The carpet raced on like a hare chased by hounds
Past orchards and meadows where cattle were grazing . . .
Past silos and barns—its speed was amazing!

Across level-crossings and bridges it sped,
Leaving behind it a trail of bright red!

"That's going to stop it!"
    the leading cop said,
When he saw them repairing
    the road up ahead.

But the carpet went WHOOSH
    past the road-mending crew.
It didn't slow down,
    but it swept on right through. . . .

STOP

MEN WOR

It knocked the sign flat
  and it sent the lamps spinning,
Just when it seemed
  the policemen were winning!

ROAD
UNDER
REPAIRS

Cruising along in their car near St. Clair,
Two cops heard a warning come over the air.
"Attention Car 4!" they heard the voice say.
"Arrest a red carpet! It's coming your way!"

BRIDGE

But they dived for the ditch—not a moment too soon—
As the carpet shot over their heads with a zoom!

And then, at a place
about two miles from Bode,

The red carpet came
to a sign in the road.

The left arm said FERRY,
the right read NEW YORK.

The carpet dashed on
and it took the left fork.

"Boys!" yelled the Police Chief.
"We'd sure better hurry!

The carpet has taken
the road to the ferry!"

Lower they crouched
and they rode faster still. . . .
But the carpet sped on
o'er the brow of the hill.

It covered the yards to the dock
    in a flash,
And it flew off the end of the slip
    with a splash;
The policemen behind
    all pulled up in a flock . . .

FERRY
50¢

Just as the ferry came into the dock!

And there on the ferryboat *Annabel Lou*
Was the Duke of Sultana and his retinue!
"My goodness!" he beamed, when he saw the display.
"This *is* a tremendous surprise I must say! . . .
A whole squad of police, and a red carpet too,
To welcome me here, from the Hotel Bellevue!"

FERRY
50¢

He shook hands with the Captain again and again,
And the Captain was just too polite to explain.
So he smiled at the Duke, and he called to his force:
  "Now that we're here, we must drive back of course!
We've finished our job, so we might just as well
  Escort the Duke back to the Bellevue Hotel!"

FERRY
50¢

So they formed up a line, two abreast in a file,
That stretched down the roadway for almost a mile!
At the head rode the policemen; their sirens were screaming. . .

At the rear rode the Duke, in his motorcar, beaming. . . .
Back they all rode, as folks cheered and waved,
On the bright scarlet path that the carpet had paved!

In village and city
the townsfolk turned out
To welcome the Duke
and his men with a shout!

Newsmen took pictures. . .
Reporters took notes. . .
Broadcasting people
got hoarse in their throats!

It was no time at all
before everyone knew
Of the carpet, the Duke,
and the Hotel Bellevue!

And the Duke himself said, as his car came to rest,

"I've had many welcomes—but this is the best!

The warmth of your greeting fills me with much cheer!

When I come to town, I shall always stay here!

And you can be sure I shall well recommend

The Bellevue Hotel to all of my friends!"

And he certainly told
every friend that he'd got!
(And he had many friends,
for he traveled a lot.)
For guests came from London,
and Paris, and Kobe,
And big towns and cities all over the globe!
And the fame of the inn spread so far and so wide
That they soon had to add a new wing on each side!

When you go to town
be sure and stay, too,

At the home of the carpet—
The Hotel Bellevue!

And you'll see the carpet
that served them so well. . .

It's the pride and the joy
of the Bellevue Hotel!

The end.